Orchard Books
A Grolier Company
95 Madison Avenue
New York, NY 10016

Manufactured in the United States of America
Printed and bound by Phoenix Color Corp.
Book design by Barbara Powderly
The text of this book is set in 18.5 Tekton MM.
The illustrations are watercolor.

Library of Congress Cataloging-in-Publication Data
Bloom, Becky.
Mice make trouble / by Becky Bloom ; illustrated by Pascal Biet. —1st American
ed.
    p.   cm.
    Summary: When Henry uses his sister's magic colored pencils to draw six mice
and a hedgehog, they all come to life and make a heap of trouble.
    ISBN 0-531-30253-9 (trade : alk. paper)
    ISBN 0-531-33253-5 (lib. bdg. : alk. paper)
    [1. Drawing Fiction. 2. Magic Fiction. 3. Mice Fiction.]
    I. Biet, Pascal, ill. II. Title.
PZ7.B62275Mi   2000   [E]—dc21   99-37708

Mice Make TROUBLE

Story by Becky Bloom

Illustrated by Pascal Biet

Orchard Books / New York

One day Henry secretly borrowed his sister's box of colored pencils. She had said the pencils were magic, and he wanted to see for himself.

"WARNING: Do not draw dangerous or mischievous animals" was printed on the cover of the box. But Henry couldn't read yet. He closed the curtains in his room and began to draw on the bare wall. He drew a tiny car and colored it red . . .

and before he had time
to draw anything else
the car popped off the
wall and zoomed across
the room. Henry would
have loved to ride in it, but the
car was way too tiny for him.
Who would be small enough to
get in this car? he wondered.

A mouse!

That was it! Henry quickly sketched a mousehole on the wall and drew a mouse above it. But the mouse didn't look quite right, and Henry had to wipe it away and draw another . . .

which wasn't right either;
neither was the next one,
or the one after that,
and so on, until six mice
had been wiped away. Henry
finally settled for a hedgehog.
It was much easier to draw.

But as the
hedgehog
walked off
the wall to
explore Henry's
room, the six
not-quite-right mice
followed right behind.
Each one of them had
the very problem that
had made Henry wipe
it away in the first place,

but none of them
seemed to mind at all.

One had too big an ear, another too long a tail, another too round a head. There were red noses, crooked whiskers, long legs, fleecy fur. What an extraordinary assortment of mice they were!

Henry was delighted to have company, but his playmates were not very civilized. They started fighting and soon spoiled the games. Only the hedgehog knew how to behave.

He had found the
colored pencils
and was drawing
a glass of soda.

Then he sat on a comfortable pillow and began to read. And that is when the trouble began. Now that the mice had found out about the magic pencils, they started drawing all sorts of toys, all of them entirely inappropriate for indoors. And they jumped and hopped and raced around the room, shrieking and cheering.

When there was no more room left to play because of all the toys, they grabbed the colored pencils and started drawing again. Earthworms and butterflies and bees and bugs of all sorts (the mice knew *not* to draw any dangerous animals) jumped off the wall and crawled and flew around the room.

What a mess they were making! Even the hedgehog contributed: his prickles had torn the pillow to pieces. Finally Henry had an idea. He grabbed the box of colored pencils away from the mice and, as fast as he could, he drew a teacher.

She was a very serious and respectable mouse-lady, with rimmed glasses and a book in her hand. And she looked just right!

"Quiet, please!" she said firmly as she walked off the wall, and at once the mice were silent and a little embarrassed. "Come to me, all of you," she instructed, taking the youngest mouse by the hand. She was about to take all of them into the mousehole and keep them busy with nursery rhymes and games.

But then she looked around Henry's room and thought it most impolite to leave him with such a mess. Taking the colored pencils, she quickly drew a broom, some soap, pails of warm water, brushes and mops.

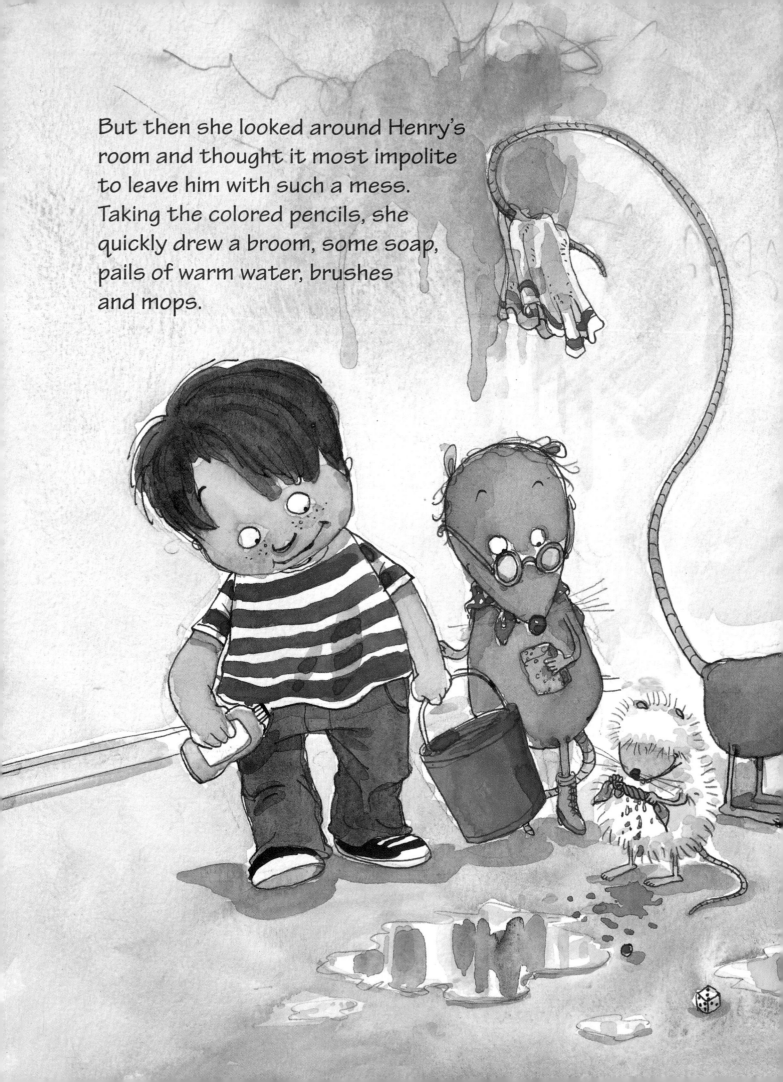

Then she had the mice and the hedgehog scrub all of the pencil marks from the walls and the floor and the furniture, and put Henry's room back in order.

And when all of the toys were put away, the teacher
drew a small cardboard box to hold all the little
animals crawling and flying about the room;
she planned to show them to her kindergarten mice.

Then the
six mice
apologized
to Henry
and went
quietly into the
mousehole.
They dragged
along the hedgehog,
who was quite
reluctant
to leave Henry's
room.

After the teacher and the animals left, there were no signs of what had happened, except for the tiny mousehole—which no one had remembered to wipe away.

And sometimes, as Henry lies in bed at night, if he listens carefully, he can still hear chuckling and giggling

coming
out of
the wall.